Alexander Graham Bell and the Telephone

Yoming S. Lin

PowerKiDS press

New York

To my two cutie bears

Published in 2012 by The Rosen Publishing Group, Inc.
29 East 21st Street, New York, NY 10010

Copyright © 2012 by The Rosen Publishing Group, Inc.

All rights reserved. No part of this book may be reproduced in any form without permission in writing from the publisher, except by a reviewer.

First Edition

Editor: Amelie von Zumbusch
Book Design: Greg Tucker

Photo Credits: Cover (Bell), pp. 6, 16, 20 (top left), 21 (top) Library of Congress/Getty Images; cover (telephone), pp. 9 (top), 12, 15 (top, bottom), 17 Science & Society Picture Library/Getty Images; p. 4 Photos.com/Thinkstock; p. 5 Hemera/Thinkstock; p. 7 (top) iStockphoto/Thinkstock; pp. 7 (bottom), 11 (top), 13 (bottom), 20 (bottom) Shutterstock.com; p. 8 © www.iStockphoto.com/David Hills; p. 9 (bottom) © www.iStockphoto.com/Pgiam; pp. 10, 13 (top) Time & Life Pictures/Mansell/Getty Images; p. 11 (bottom) Jupiterimages/Creatas/Thinkstock; p. 14 Kean Collection/Getty Images; p. 18 Dr. Gilbert H. Grosvenor/National Geographic/Getty Images; p. 19 Anne Revis Grosvenor/National Geographic/Getty Images; p. 20 (top right) Stock Montage/Getty Images; p. 21 (bottom) Rolls Press/Popperfoto/Getty Images.

Library of Congress Cataloging-in-Publication Data

Lin, Yoming S.
 Alexander Graham Bell and the telephone / by Yoming S. Lin. — 1st ed.
   p. cm. — (Eureka!)
 Includes index.
 ISBN 978-1-4488-5034-1 (library binding)
 1. Bell, Alexander Graham, 1847–1922—Juvenile literature. 2. Inventors—United States—Biography—Juvenile literature. 3. Telephone—United States—History—Juvenile literature. I. Title.
 TK6143.B4L546 2012
 621.385092—dc22
 [B]
                              2011006088

Manufactured in the United States of America

CPSIA Compliance Information: Batch #WS11PK: For Further Information contact Rosen Publishing, New York, New York at 1-800-237-9932

Contents

Bell's Big Idea	4
Bell's Childhood	6
Growing Up	8
Moving to the United States	10
Exciting Discovery	12
The Telephone	14
More Interesting Work	16
Bell's Greatest Gift	18
Timeline	20
Inside the Science	22
Glossary	23
Index	24
Web Sites	24

Bell's Big Idea

If you talked on the phone today, you can thank Alexander Graham Bell. He invented the telephone in the nineteenth century. He was born in Scotland and later moved to North America.

Bell was interested in sounds and **speech**, or the act of speaking, starting at an early age. This would lead him to

Bell was a very curious person. He kept on inventing things even after the telephone had made him rich and famous.

How often do you talk on the telephone? Today, telephones are a big part of most peoples' lives. However, they have been around for under 150 years.

his most famous discovery. He figured out how to use **electricity** to get sounds to travel a long way. Bell used this science to build his telephone.

Bell changed the way people stay in touch with each other. For the first time, people could talk to friends without leaving their homes!

Bell's Childhood

Bell was born in Edinburgh, Scotland, in 1847. His mother, Eliza Symonds Bell, was deaf. His father, Alexander Melville Bell, was called Melville. Melville studied speech. Young Alexander liked to read and write. Like his father, he

This picture of Bell was taken when he was 14 or 15 years old. Bell's friends and family called him Aleck. In later years, he would spell his nickname Alec.

was interested in speech. He tried to figure out the best way to talk to his mother. He spoke with a low voice near her forehead. He guessed that his voice made **vibrations**, or back and forth movements, that let her hear him somewhat. He was right!

Alexander was the middle child of three brothers. As kids, the brothers built a machine that made speaking sounds.

Top: Bell went to Edinburgh's Royal High School, seen here, for several years. *Bottom*: Edinburgh, where Bell was born and grew up, is the capital of Scotland.

Growing Up

At 16 years old, Alexander started teaching music and **elocution**, or the control of one's voice. The Bell brothers traveled around Scotland teaching their father's Visible Speech system. This used symbols to teach deaf people how to move their mouths to produce speech.

For a while, Bell took classes at Edinburgh's University of Edinburgh, seen here. He also studied at the University of London, in London, England.

A few years later, Bell read the German scientist Hermann von Helmholtz's work. Helmholtz described using electrical tools to make certain speech sounds. This made Bell think about electricity and sound.

Sadly, both of Bell's brothers died of the sickness **tuberculosis** when they were young adults. Bell got tuberculosis, too. He moved to Canada with his family in 1870. They hoped he would get better there, and he did.

Top: Helmholtz, seen here, worked in several branches of science. *Bottom*: The Bell family bought this house soon after moving to Brantford, in Ontario, Canada.

Moving to the United States

In 1871, Bell moved to Boston, Massachusetts. There, he taught Visible Speech to deaf students. One of his students was Mabel Hubbard. They would later fall in love.

Bell continued studying speech. He made a machine that drew **sound**

This picture of students and teachers at the Horace Mann School for the Deaf and Hard of Hearing was taken in 1871. It is one of several schools where Bell (top right) taught.

waves, or air vibrations, made by his voice. While studying sound waves, Bell had an idea. He knew that **electric currents**, or electricity flowing through wires, could travel long distances. If he could get electric currents to vibrate like sound waves, the currents could carry sounds over long distances.

Bell also studied the electric **telegraph**. People used this to send messages to people who lived far away. The telegraph sent messages with electric signals.

Top: This is what sound waves look like drawn on a modern machine. *Bottom*: All sounds, including a friend's whisper, travel through the air as sound waves.

Exciting Discovery

Bell started to experiment with telegraphs. A telegraph could send only one message at a time. Bell wanted to get it to send many messages at once. Bell set up a telegraph, with the part that sent messages in one room and the part that received

Before Bell hired him, Watson worked at an electrical machine shop. After the telephone made both men rich, Watson traveled, started a shipbuilding company, and took up acting.

them in another. One day, Bell's assistant, Thomas Watson, was fixing part of the telegraph. Bell heard a sound come through the part of the telegraph in the other room. It sounded like a person's voice. Bell wondered if he could use electricity to carry the sounds of voices. He started building a telephone. Bell got a **patent** for his invention. This meant he was the only person who could make and sell telephones.

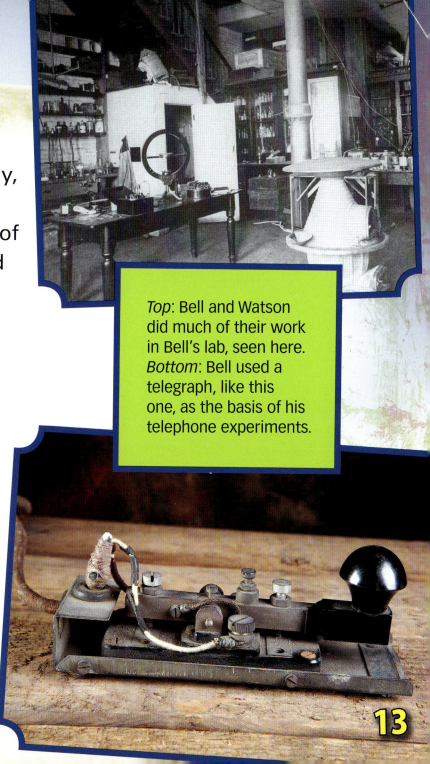

Top: Bell and Watson did much of their work in Bell's lab, seen here. *Bottom*: Bell used a telegraph, like this one, as the basis of his telephone experiments.

The Telephone

On March 10, 1876, Bell spoke into his telephone to test his invention. A telephone **transmitter** turned sound waves from his voice into electric currents. The currents traveled down the wire toward the telephone **receiver**, which Watson was holding in another room. The receiver turned the electric currents back into sound waves, which

The World's Fair where Bell showed his telephone was known as the Centennial Exhibition. It took place in the United States' centennial, or hundredth, year as a country.

traveled to Watson's ear. Watson could hear Bell's voice!

Bell brought his invention to the 1876 World's Fair, in Philadelphia, Pennsylvania. It was a success. Two years later, President Rutherford B. Hayes had his own telephone! In 1877, Bell helped form the Bell Telephone Company. It would grow into one of the largest companies in the United States.

Top: Bell showed this improved version of his telephone transmitter at the 1876 World's Fair. *Bottom*: Bell's first telephone used a liquid transmitter.

More Interesting Work

Bell married Mabel Hubbard in July 1877. They went on to have four children together. Their family lived in the United States most of the year but spent summers at their home in Nova Scotia, Canada.

By the time Bell was in his early thirties, he was rich and successful. Many people were starting to use telephones in their houses. However, Bell

Here Bell is with his wife and their daughters, Elsie (left) and Marian (second from right). Marian was called Daisy. Sadly, the Bells' two sons died as babies.

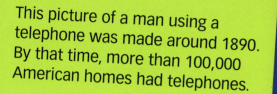

This picture of a man using a telephone was made around 1890. By that time, more than 100,000 American homes had telephones.

continued to work hard. He invented a metal detector, a tool that sensed the presence of metal. He worked with kites and **hydrofoils**, a type of boat, to study motion in air and water. Bell even invented a photophone, which used light instead of electricity to get sounds to travel long distances.

Bell's Greatest Gift

Bell continued to work on ways to help teach deaf people to communicate for the rest of his life. He also helped start *National Geographic*, a magazine about the natural world. Bell died on August 2, 1922, at his summer home in Nova Scotia.

Bell will always be remembered for his work on the telephone. Almost

This picture shows Bell (holding a baby) and his family, including several grandchildren, at their summer home in Nova Scotia.

Bell named his house in Nova Scotia Beinn Bhreagh. This means "beautiful mountain," in Scottish Gaelic, a language from Scotland. The house is on Cape Breton Island.

100 years after his death, the science behind Bell's telephone and photophone are still the basis of our phones, the Internet, and even cable television. However, Bell's greatest gift may have been letting us easily stay in touch with loved ones, even when they live halfway around the world!

Timeline

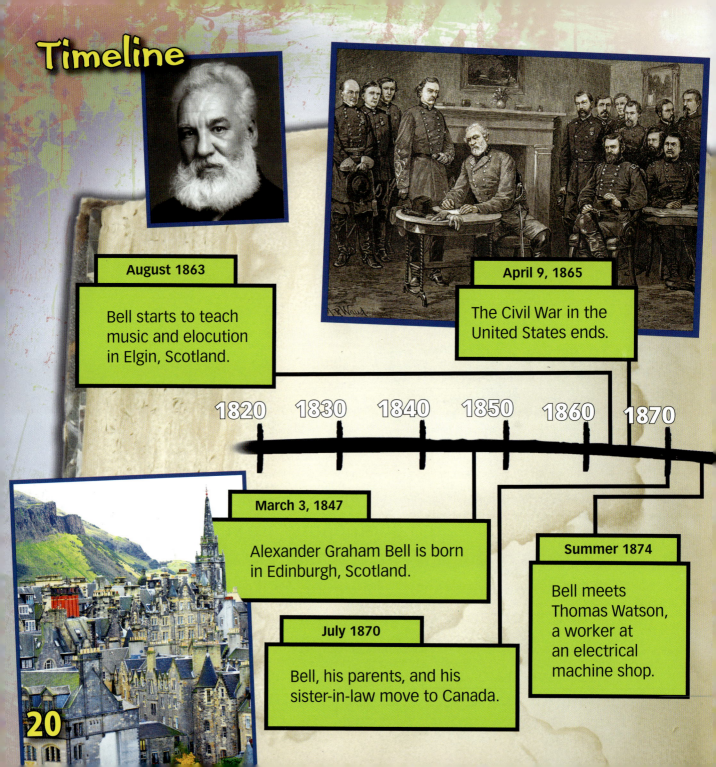

August 1863
Bell starts to teach music and elocution in Elgin, Scotland.

April 9, 1865
The Civil War in the United States ends.

1820 1830 1840 1850 1860 1870

March 3, 1847
Alexander Graham Bell is born in Edinburgh, Scotland.

July 1870
Bell, his parents, and his sister-in-law move to Canada.

Summer 1874
Bell meets Thomas Watson, a worker at an electrical machine shop.

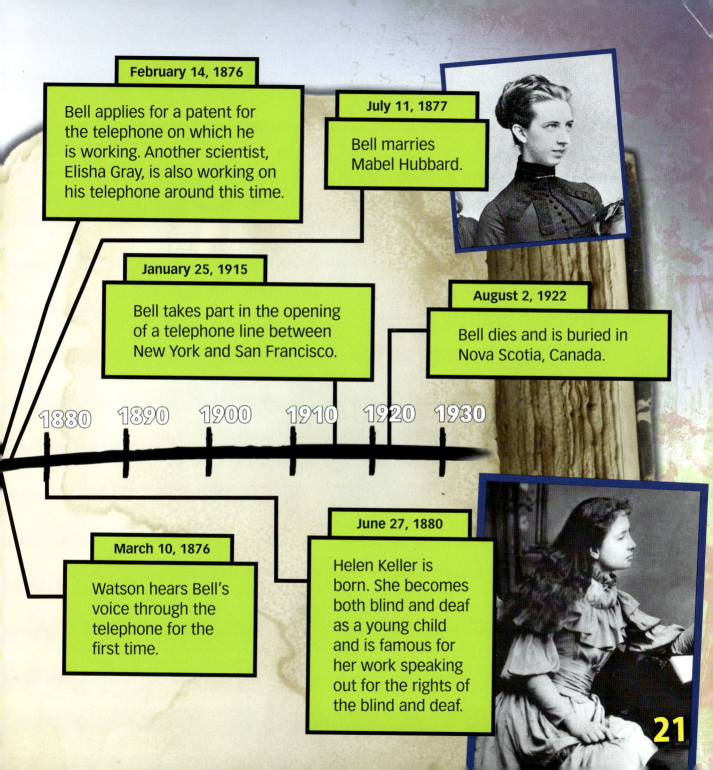

Inside the Science

1. A telegraph uses electric currents traveling across a wire to send codes across distances. The electric currents arrive on a machine that turns them into clicking sounds. Someone who has been trained to understand the code then figures out the message.

2. When we speak, our voices make air move back and forth. This forms sound waves. Different sounds make waves with different shapes.

3. When a person talked into Bell's telephone, the sound waves made a small metal plate move back and forth. The plate hit an **electromagnet**, or a magnet made by electric currents. This caused an electric current to flow down a wire. The current made an electromagnet in the receiver at the other end of the wire vibrate. This made sound waves someone could hear.

4. Sound traveled on a beam of light in Bell's photophone. A person's voice was directed at a mirror, and the mirror vibrated from the sound waves. Then, sunlight was pointed at the mirror to catch these vibrations. Our modern telephone system, the Internet, and cable TV are based on this science.

Glossary

electric currents (ih-LEK-trik KUR-ents) Flows of electricity.

electricity (ih-lek-TRIH-suh-tee) Power that produces light, heat, or movement.

electromagnet (ih-lek-troh-MAG-net) A magnet made by electricity.

elocution (eh-luh-KYOO-shun) The art of speaking well.

hydrofoils (HY-druh-foy-ulz) Boats with winglike parts that raise them out of the water.

patent (PA-tent) A document that stops people from copying an invention.

receiver (rih-SEE-ver) The part of a telephone into which a person talks.

sound waves (SOWND WAYVZ) The movements of sound through the air.

speech (SPEECH) The act of talking.

telegraph (TEH-lih-graf) A machine used to send messages through wires using coded signals.

transmitter (trants-MIH-ter) The part of a telephone out of which sound comes.

tuberculosis (too-ber-kyuh-LOH-sis) A sickness that affects the lungs.

vibrations (vy-BRAY-shunz) Fast movements up and down or back and forth.

Index

B
Bell, Eliza Symonds (mother), 6–7

E
Edinburgh, Scotland, 6, 20
electric current(s), 11, 14, 22
electricity, 5, 9, 11, 13, 17
electromagnet, 22

F
friends, 5

H
home(s), 5, 16, 18
hydrofoils, 17

I
invention, 13–15

N
North America, 4

P
patent, 13, 21

R
receiver, 14, 22

S
science, 5, 19, 22
sound(s), 4–5, 7, 9, 11, 13, 17, 22
sound waves, 10–11, 14, 22
speech, 4, 6–8, 10

T
telegraph(s), 11–13, 22
transmitter, 14
tuberculosis, 9

V
vibrations, 7, 11, 22

Web Sites

Due to the changing nature of Internet links, PowerKids Press has developed an online list of Web sites related to the subject of this book. This site is updated regularly. Please use this link to access the list: www.powerkidslinks.com/eure/bell/